My Amazing Diary 2021

Little Treasures

Edited By Debbie Killingworth

First published in Great Britain in 2021 by:

◊ YoungWriters®
— Est. 1991 —

Young Writers
Remus House
Coltsfoot Drive
Peterborough
PE2 9BF
Telephone: 01733 890066
Website: www.youngwriters.co.uk

All Rights Reserved
Book Design by Ashley Janson
© Copyright Contributors 2021
Softback ISBN 978-1-80015-605-0

Printed and bound in the UK by BookPrintingUK
Website: www.bookprintinguk.com
YB0484X

Foreword

Dear Reader,

You will never guess what I did today! Shall I tell you? Some primary school pupils wrote some diary entries and I got to read them, and they were **excellent!**

They wrote them in school and sent them to us here at Young Writers. We'd given their teachers some bright and funky worksheets to fill in, and some fun and fabulous (and free) resources to help spark ideas and get inspiration flowing.

And it clearly worked because **WOW!!** I can't believe the adventures I've been reading about. Real people, make believe people, dogs and unicorns, even objects like pencils all feature and these diaries all have one thing in common – they are **jam-packed** with imagination!

We live and breathe creativity here at Young Writers – it gives us life! We want to pass our love of the written word onto the next generation and what better way to do that than to celebrate their writing by publishing it in a book!

It sets their work free from homework books and notepads and puts it where it deserves to be – **out in the world!** Each awesome author in this book should be **super proud** of themselves, and now they've got proof of their imagination, their ideas and their creativity in black and white, to look back on in years to come!

Now that I've read all these diaries, I've somehow got to pick some winners! Oh my gosh it's going to be difficult to choose, but I'm going to have **so much fun** doing it!

Bye!

Debbie

Contents

Deepdene School, Hove

Tess Carter (8)	1
Arya Dauris-Ames (7)	2
Jasmine Morgan (7)	4
Mia Broadstock (7)	6
Louis Hallam (7)	7
Scarlett Goble (7)	8
Sid Granger-Hughes (6)	9
Harley Ford (7)	10

Hill Top CE Primary School, Low Moor

Keiron Pattison (5)	11
Jorge Day (6)	12
Joshua Shaw (6)	13
Alyssa Godfrey (6)	14
Jacob Whitrick (6)	15
Donnie Royle (6)	16
Bobby Hegarty (6)	17
Jack Hunter (6)	18
Olly Marshall	19
Lilly Davies (6)	20
Norah Maloney (6)	21
El Mehdaoui (7)	22
Frankie Butterfield (6)	23
Verity Mullen (5)	24

Krishna Avanti Primary School, Evington

Dylan Lad (7)	25
Mehul Chotai (7)	26
Srija Choudhuri (7)	28
Ridhi Modwadia (7)	30
Ria Bokhiria (6)	32
Arjun Bhatt (7)	33
Manya Patel (7)	34
Jaslyn Kaur (8)	35
Kavir Sheth (7)	36
Disha Bokhiriya (7)	37
Kiesha Patel (7)	38
Vanshika Mankad (7)	39
Visva Visvavisvavadiya (7)	40
Samar Gudka (7)	41
Moksha Parekh (7)	42
Sahil Chudasama (7)	43
Avi Mistry (7)	44
Soham Bhutiya (7)	45
Riya Kumar (7)	46
Amber Patel (7)	47
Kaylan Gohil (7)	48
Aarohi Brahmbhatt (8)	49
Nieve Patel (7)	50
Raya Patel (7)	51
Nikunj Sevak (6)	52
Radhika Szamocka (7)	53
Adi Jani (7)	54
Mohan Lokesh (6)	55
Kushal Desai (7)	56
Srijit Choudhuri (7)	57
Aashika Anand (7)	58
Shivam Dhamecha (7)	59
Aarna Patel (6)	60
Pranav Patel (7)	61
Tia Odedra (6)	62
Ania Chauhan (7)	63
Mia Gohil (6)	64
Jasmine Budwal (7)	65
Dhruva Devabala (7)	66

Keya Tailor (7)	67
Dylan Bhundia (7)	68
Shay Pankhania (6)	69
Siya Odedara (7)	70
Kian Peshawaria (6)	71
Veda-Shruti Mistry (7)	72
Hanaya Kotecha (7)	73

Lever Edge Primary Academy, Bolton

Zara Imran (7)	74
Wei Qi Chen (7)	76
Aisha Waqar (7)	78
Lama Abo (7)	80
Adeena Ishaq (7)	81
Haidar Khan (7)	82

Plantation Primary School, Halewood

Eliza Kotti (6)	83
Chloe Budd (7)	84
Amber Duffy (7)	85
Cianna Rainey (7)	86
Chloe Williams (8)	87
Matilda Bate (7)	88
Nylah Ritchie (7)	89
Luca Jones (7)	90
Alice Logan (7)	91
Robyn Ross-Forth (6)	92
Evelyn McNally (6)	93
Evie Sunners (7)	94
Jack Mcstein (7)	95
Bobby Steele (7)	96
Sofia Bayliss (7)	97
Heidi Hanson (7)	98

Thornborough Infant School, Thornborough

Romilly Withers (7)	99

Upminster Infant School, Upminster

Harley Craig (7)	100
Oliver Humphrey (7)	102
Kaya Shah (7)	104
Iggy Cox (7)	106
George Jaques (7)	108
Parker Brannigan Warren (7)	110
Lottie Hindley (7)	112
Albie Dickinson (7)	113
Jack Fryer (7)	114
Ben (7)	115
Isabel Burdett (7)	116
Ellie Winston (7)	117
Sophia Aherne (7)	118
Joseph Walters (7)	119
Jaden Thurston (7)	120
Torben Barr (6)	121
Reeva King (6)	122
Freya Webb (7)	123
Hollie Kitchener (7)	124
Henry Davidson (6)	125
Cecily Lloyd (6)	126
Sienna Woodhurst (7)	127
Xanthia Groom (7)	128
Harry Cheek (7)	129
David Ryan (7)	130
Emily Walder (7)	131
Poppy Fleet (7)	132
Eniola Orisatoki (6)	133
Joshua Quilter (6)	134
Sophia Crocker (7)	135
Ruby Trew (6)	136
James Bailey (7)	137
Eden Mackenzie-Smith (7)	138
Finlay Hardy (7)	139
Alice Pepper (7)	140
Henry Francis (7)	141
Lexia Napier Deutsher (7)	142
Bertram Moore (7)	143
Freya Bourne (7)	144
Kyle Sagisi (6)	145

Wraysbury Primary School, Wraysbury

Emin Mehmet-Khan (6)	146
Zoya Hayat (6)	147
Kairan Kharay (6)	148
Grace Kirby (6)	149
Beau Loveridge (6)	150
Sophia Bedford (6)	151
Eva Shurman (5)	152
Aidan Woollard (6)	153
Harrison Cowie (6)	154
Lexi Burke (6)	155
Rehaan Mian (6)	156
Renzo Assi (6)	157
Ikonkar Gill-Mangat (6)	158
Azaan Ali (6)	159
Priya Basra (6)	160
Freya McKenzie (6)	161
Ava Kirby (6)	162
Darcie Taggart (6)	163
Rion Agrawal (6)	164
Ikraj Matharoo (6)	165
Lottie Connolly (6)	166
Luke Richens (6)	167
Shaniyal Mahmood (6)	168
Michael Harris (6)	169
Ralphie Croft (6)	170
Oliwia Lubinska (6)	171

The Diaries

Dear Diary

During the weekend, I went to a cool funfair! I met my best friend, Ernie, who is so much fun and we went on the carousel and it was really fast. Next, we played some games. The first game was called 'it', It was so much fun. Then we left and went to the park. My friend played on the slide. It was wet so we got a tissue and cleaned the slide. Then we had lunch and it was yummy. Next, we played on the swings but they were too slow so we played on something else called a hippo ride. It made us feel sick! Then we went home and had a roast dinner. It was yummy! After that, we played a game called 'trickster'. Ernie won and I lost. Then we had a party and there was cake!

Tess Carter (8)
Deepdene School, Hove

Dear Diary

On Saturday, I got a great opportunity to meet the person I look up to... Lilly James and we went to Oradon. Me and Lilly James were in the library. I pulled a book but the book did not come out. "Oh," I said as I fell to the ground. But suddenly the book turned around... It shouted.
"Riddle!" we both shouted.
It said, "It's something white up in the sky. It holds rain and wind. Good luck because you don't have long."
"B-b-but..." I tried to explain but it would not listen.
"It's in the sky and holds wind and rain" repeated Lilly James.
I followed what she said. "Clouds, it has to be!" we both said.
"You are right, well done for succeeding in your task," said the voice.

"I know, we can shoot a movie!" said Lilly James.
"That's a great idea," I said.
"Let's get shooting!" we both said with enjoyment.
Bye Diary.

Arya Dauris-Ames (7)
Deepdene School, Hove

Dear Diary

On Sunday, I went to the zoo. I saw a unicorn and a chinchilla with my friend, Pokémon. He's funny. Next, we went to an epic funfair and went on amazing rides. Next, we went to the park, it was so epic, we went on the amazing slide and swing, epic! Then we went home. Me and Pokémon had chocolate and watched TV, played computer games and went horse riding. Next, we went home and did art and 'Just Dance' and went to bed and had a midnight feast. The next day me and Pokémon had a milkshake and sweets for breakfast and saw a fairy. It was so cool and epic, it had lots of powers, it had a pet dragon. The dragon breathed fire and water and Pokémon couldn't believe its eyes! He screamed, "Help me!"

I said, "Sure, it's a nice dragon, isn't that right Fairy?"
"Yes!" it said and so we went to bed.

Jasmine Morgan (7)
Deepdene School, Hove

Dear Diary

On Saturday, I went to Snowflake Waters. It was as cold as the Arctic with crashing waves. I went with my fierce friend, Bella, she can beat up anything! I said, "Have you got a coat?"
"Yes."
But instead, a unicorn came, it was called Bluebell, it had lovely soft wings. A little pixie was flying next to it, its name was Snowy, it had a dress made from petals. Bluebell, me, Bella and Snowy went for a swim, it was much warmer. We met the Queen of Ice, she was really pretty. We had a smoothie. It was yummy. I rode Bluebell home and I played with her. I had some dinner and went flying. She did awesome tricks and I said, "Best day ever!"

Mia Broadstock (7)
Deepdene School, Hove

Dear Diary

On Monday, I went to football and I travelled in a football portal with Tess, it was very fun. We went to Candy Land. Me and Tess found another portal and went to the funfair. We went on a roller coaster, a dragon one, it was amazing. The dragon was real! We went, "Argh!" He was friendly though. We captured him for a pet and named him Fred. We got cotton candy for the dragon, it was the best bank holiday ever. After, I went swimming, it was super and amazing!

Louis Hallam (7)
Deepdene School, Hove

Dear Diary

On Saturday, I went to the funfair with my friend, Jasmine, she is hilarious. We went on a bumper car, it was really fun. When we were done we got a McDonald's and it was delicious then we took Jasmine home.
On Sunday I went horse riding and the horse's name is Leo. I rode Leo on the road, he is also really tall. After, I rode him back to his stable and flew back home because I'm a fairy and I got into bed and went to sleep.

Scarlett Goble (7)
Deepdene School, Hove

Dear Diary

Monday, I went to space. I went with my family and friends. In space, I found a zoo and a park. I explored the park. We saw a slide and a swing then we went to the zoo. I saw an alien. Next, we flew back to Earth. The next day, we went back to space. We went to the zoo and I saw one thing... I saw an emu.

Sid Granger-Hughes (6)
Deepdene School, Hove

Dear Diary

During the weekend, I went to the piggy funfair and a bear took me and a superhero to space. I was happy, proud and pleased. Then a monster took me to the zoo. After that, the superhero took me to the park. What a busy day!

Harley Ford (7)
Deepdene School, Hove

Dear Diary

I went to Blackpool.
I went to the park.
I went to the arcade.
I went to the rock pool.
I went to the zoo.
I went to the funfair. I went on the rides.
I went to the beach.
I went to the park.

Keiron Pattison (5)
Hill Top CE Primary School, Low Moor

Dear Diary

I went to the caravan with my family. When I was there I went to the funfair and I was always smiling. When I got back from the funfair I played computer games and I went to the park. I had a happy weekend at the caravan.

Jorge Day (6)
Hill Top CE Primary School, Low Moor

Dear Diary

I went to the zoo.
I met a superhero.
I went to space and I saw the moon.
I went to the park. I went on the swing.
I went with my family.
I went to the funfair.
I went to the farm.

Joshua Shaw (6)
Hill Top CE Primary School, Low Moor

Dear Diary

I went to my friend's house and we went to the park.
I went to the beach at Blackpool.
I went on the slides and I went to play football.
I went to space and I went to my sister's house.

Alyssa Godfrey (6)
Hill Top CE Primary School, Low Moor

Dear Diary

I played football with a tiger. Then I played basketball with the tiger. I won the game. Then I went to the seaside and got a bucket and spade. I went for a paddle in the sea with wavy rocks and shiny shells.

Jacob Whitrick (6)
Hill Top CE Primary School, Low Moor

Dear Diary

I went to London and I saw a skyscraper then I went to my dark, secret, underground ninja base. I had the most awesome base. I saw a flying tiger. It flew to space. It was cool.

Donnie Royle (6)
Hill Top CE Primary School, Low Moor

Dear Diary

I went to space with my best friend, Lilly and I saw an alien.
I went to the cinema with my family to watch Peter Rabbit 2.
I went to the beach with my family.

Bobby Hegarty (6)
Hill Top CE Primary School, Low Moor

Dear Diary

I went to the park.

I went to space. I went to Mars. I saw an alien on Mars. The alien bounced around and it jumped onto the moon. Then he bounced back onto Mars.

Jack Hunter (6)
Hill Top CE Primary School, Low Moor

Dear Diary

I went to the ball pit with my brother and sister. I played in the ball pit and we had fun then we went on the trampoline. We jumped high and did a backflip.

Olly Marshall
Hill Top CE Primary School, Low Moor

Dear Diary

I went to the park with my best friend, Bobby. We played on the swings and the slide. I went to the cinema to watch Peter Rabbit 2. I had lots of fun.

Lilly Davies (6)
Hill Top CE Primary School, Low Moor

Dear Diary

I went to the park.
I went to see my friend.
I went on holiday.
I went home.
I had a nice time.
I met my friends.

Norah Maloney (6)
Hill Top CE Primary School, Low Moor

Dear Diary

I went to London and I saw my uncle.
I went to the park.
I went to space and I saw an alien. They helped me get back home.

El Mehdaoui (7)
Hill Top CE Primary School, Low Moor

Dear Diary

I went to the fair. I went on the rides. I went on a roller coaster. I saw my cousin at the funfair. I saw William at the funfair.

Frankie Butterfield (6)
Hill Top CE Primary School, Low Moor

Dear Diary

I went to space. I met some aliens that live there. When I was going home I said goodbye. I went back home.

Verity Mullen (5)
Hill Top CE Primary School, Low Moor

Dear Diary

Today, I was doing my homework then I decided to go to my friend's house but my friend was already at my door. He came in and we talked. Then we decided to go outside but when we stepped out there was a mysterious ocean. It had magically appeared in our city so we bravely dived in and saw lots of beautiful coral. Also, we saw a spectacular narwhal and some funny clownfish. They looped around. We swam on but a really nasty shark swam behind us but luckily we are very fast swimmers. When we swam the shark got tired so easily. Then we saw a treasure chest. It didn't belong in the ocean so we took it and swam up. Magically the ocean disappeared and the ground turned back into grass and mud. We were soaked. My friend went back home. I was so curious I opened the chest, it was full of gold.

Dylan Lad (7)
Krishna Avanti Primary School, Evington

Dear Diary

Last week I went on holiday. I will tell you all about what I did. It was all about going to Spain and riding a horse. I went with my three friends, Ari, Sahil and Nomit. We went in the morning at 9am before breakfast. Next to our hotel was a café so we had breakfast there. I had two hash browns, scrambled egg, beans and a vegetable sausage. Ari had two hash browns, egg and beans. Sahil had one hash brown and two helpings of egg. Finally, Nomit had beans and egg.

After breakfast, we went to a shop that hired sports cars. Nomit went for an epic convertible, Ari and Sahil went in a black and red striped Porsche. I went for a green Lamborghini. When we reached where we were going we parked our cars in the parking station. We walked for two minutes to reach the pony den. The ponies were all sorts of colours like black, white and brown.

They had lots of stuff and they had bushy tails wagging behind them. When we went on the horses they were a bit bumpy. Before we left we got to say thank you. Then we swapped our vehicles and as we were tired we slept. It was the best day of my life!

Mehul Chotai (7)
Krishna Avanti Primary School, Evington

Dear Diary

Last weekend, I did something really exciting! I went on a safari. I went with my mum, dad, brother and sister. We went on cycles. We took colouring pencils, rubbers, rulers, binoculars, paper and windcheaters. On the safari, we saw a giant, scary tiger. It was hunting zebras. One zebra behind the tree was very scared. I quickly drew and coloured in a picture of them. At lunchtime, we had pizza and chips and my brother and I had candyfloss. As it was a hot day, we had vanilla ice cream and chocolate brownies.

Afterwards, we saw a female lion hunting small animals. Should I tell you a fact I know about lions? I will! Only female lions hunt! I drew a picture of them also. When we stopped for a water break we saw a brown monkey walking towards us.

It was throwing bananas everywhere. It was my favourite day ever!

Srija Choudhuri (7)
Krishna Avanti Primary School, Evington

Dear Diary

Today, I went to the zoo with my mum, dad and my little sister. I went to the zoo because it's very fascinating seeing the animals. First, we went to see the funny monkeys eating yellow bananas in the high trees. Next, we went to see the blue elephants, they splashed the water on the dusty windows. Finally, we went to see the lions, they had sharp teeth, razor-sharp claws and big bushy tails. Suddenly a big blue monster came out of a bush. It had big, monstrous claws, red eyes and a big blue tummy. The monster started attacking the animals, eating their food but then two determined superheroes came flying down from the sky. They used their powers to shrink the monster and the silly monster ran away.

Me and my family came home and had a good night's sleep. I hope I get to talk to you again. See you soon.

Ridhi Modwadia (7)
Krishna Avanti Primary School, Evington

Dear Diary

Today, I went to the park alone. I went to swing and then the swing got higher, higher, and higher. Then it swung me near a magical tree. I went around the swing and on the tree, I saw a door. I opened the door and inside it, there was a mythical world, inside it was a house. I went inside the house bravely and there was a shadow and then a monster. I was about to run away then the monster waved then I realised that the monster was friendly. I took the monster to my land.

The monster followed me everywhere I went. I also took the monster to my house and school and almost everywhere. Once I took the monster to the playground on the swing and suddenly the monster disappeared back into its world and I never forgot the friendly, cuddly monster again.

Ria Bokhiria (6)
Krishna Avanti Primary School, Evington

Dear Diary

One year ago, I went on holiday with my brothers, mum and dad. My dad had to buy a room for us. We paid for our room then the manager gave my dad the keys to the room. I was amazed when I went into the room, it was huge!

The first thing we did was we went to the water park. There was a huge bucket at the top. When it was full of water the bucket splashed water all over me. After that I had ice cream then I got all dry.

The next day, I woke up and we had breakfast at the café. I ate some eggs and watermelon. After that, I played some football with my brothers then I went on a floaty in the pool. I climbed up the stairs and went on the slide. In the slide there were lights. That was the best holiday ever!

Arjun Bhatt (7)
Krishna Avanti Primary School, Evington

Dear Diary

Today at Hogwarts, Ron and I found out that Harry was being troubled by Voldemort. His scar burned so much that he was being weakened and Harry felt very, very weak. So, it was up to Ron and me to save Harry. In order to save Harry, Ron and I had to find the golden cup Horcrux. "But how will we get there without being attacked by Aragog, the mighty spider?" Ron whined.
"Oh let's just ask Dobby to teleport us into Beatrix's vault," I said.
So we called Dobby. He teleported us there but before Ron and I could get in, Ron touched the golden plate so the whole vault flooded. Finally, when we were still we could fly on our brooms and get to Hogwarts.

Manya Patel (7)
Krishna Avanti Primary School, Evington

Dear Diary

A few weeks ago, I went to Abbey Park. I went with my mum and brother. I didn't know that Abbey Park has a traditional Chinese bridge. It also has a flower garden. I saw a big water fountain, it looked majestic! They had chains around it for some reason. The best part was that inside trees were little gaps to stand in, we also saw a tree that was shaped like a bench. We sat on the tree and took many photos. After a while, we were so tired that we sat underneath a mammoth-sized tree and took a rest. Then, after twenty minutes, my mum said, "Let's go home because I'm hungry, you also must be starving too." Finally, after an exhausting day, we all went home.

Jaslyn Kaur (8)
Krishna Avanti Primary School, Evington

Dear Diary

Today was the best day of my life. I was running rapidly with Krish then I met a strange-looking clown. He invited us to a circus but he hesitated. He said, "Terrible, awful circus that captures animals, um... I actually meant to say good circus. Anyway will you come?" he asked curiously.
I said, "I don't believe you."
Krish said, "Yes, let's go."
While we were arguing a big cage dropped on us and the clown revealed himself. He was actually a hunter who loved flesh. We tried to escape desperately then suddenly a good fox appeared and he tore the net and we were free. We ran as fast as our legs could take us.

Kavir Sheth (7)
Krishna Avanti Primary School, Evington

Dear Diary

A few days ago, I kept on asking my parents to play with me but they refused to play. I was bored out of my mind, in fact, I was super duper bored. I kept on staring at the glass window in silence until I saw a mysterious door as long as a giraffe. I headed to the door and opened it with excitement, it was a magical forest! I also brought my brother along with me. I went inside and it was magnificent and beautiful. I decided to make a swing out of the ropes. Suddenly, I saw some fairy dust that was prettier than glitter. I actually realised that it was Tinkerbell and Peter Pan. We did many fun things together and it was a great day but I had to come home.

Disha Bokhiriya (7)
Krishna Avanti Primary School, Evington

Dear Diary

You won't believe what I did at the weekend. At the weekend I went to the zoo. I went with my mum, dad and brother. It was really sunny so my mum and dad let me have ice cream. I had a slushie but my brother had an ice lolly. When we got there we had to give some tickets to the zookeeper. The first animal we saw was a crocodile that had big, scary and yellow teeth. At lunchtime, we ate some chips and a burger. I had a chocolate milkshake with it.

The last animal we saw was a hippo and it was huge. It made a big splash. We all got wet so we came home, got changed and went to bed. It was the best day of my life.

Kiesha Patel (7)
Krishna Avanti Primary School, Evington

Dear Diary

I had a mysterious day today. I was playing with my friend, Mocksha in the gardens. We were playing our favourite game of hide-and-seek. Suddenly we found a mysterious hole. We were walking around it until I fell in. I tried to get hold of Mocksha's hand but she fell in too! We fell deeper and deeper into the hole. It led us to a zoo! We were clueless. Why would someone bad go to a zoo? We looked everywhere and found the culprit. A very dangerous culprit. It was a tiger. Then we shot off like a rocket. Suddenly Mocksha found a crystal and we were back home. "What an adventure!" I said.

Vanshika Mankad (7)
Krishna Avanti Primary School, Evington

Dear Diary

I went to the beach with my dad, mum, brother and cousins. We went yesterday. We went in a big grey car. When we got there we played in the soft fluffy sand, it was like play-dough. My cousin said, "Look in the ocean!"
We looked and saw something sparkling like the sun. My brother said, "Is it a mermaid?" My cousin said, "Yes!"
"Is that treasure?"
"Yes!" said my cousin.
It was real. The mermaid went away but left shells glistening and sparkly water behind. The sun went but the colours were shining like glittery water.

Visva Visvavisvavadiya (7)
Krishna Avanti Primary School, Evington

Dear Diary

Yesterday, I went to the beach with my family. It took two hours and fifty minutes to get there by car. The beach was called Great Yarmouth. We played football. We were there for four hours. We swam for ten minutes then we ate some yummy ice cream. The flavour of the ice cream was chocolate. After going to the beach we went to the funfair and went on lots of rides. My favourite ride was like a roller coaster, it was fast and very scary. After that, we went to a restaurant and had some pizza and came home. I went in the shower and went to bed. I had the best day ever.

Samar Gudka (7)
Krishna Avanti Primary School, Evington

Dear Diary

Today, I went into my garden. Suddenly the bell rang and I flung open the door. It was Aarohi. Soon the magical chalk glittered, which meant it was time for adventure. We drew a door which came to life! She was amazed! So, anyways, we stepped in and it led us to a magical world. Suddenly the bushes rustled. We were frightened but to our surprise there was Aladdin. He had been lost for two weeks he explained. Then he had an idea, he could go on his magical carpet. So we jumped on and had a wonky ride. By the time we were back, it was time to go home.

Moksha Parekh (7)
Krishna Avanti Primary School, Evington

Dear Diary

You would not believe what happened. Two days ago, when I was asleep, a superhero flew down to Earth. He hit his head on my roof while flying down.
The superhero then landed on the ground. His name was Sunitam. Sunitam broke some cupboards as he carried my house. It made the loudest noise I ever heard. I woke up with amazement. Sunitam did not recognise me. I was wobbling and I kept on falling down. I was fed up with it so I jumped out of the house. I told Sunitam to stop. Sunitam put the house down and flew away. Then I went back to sleep.

Sahil Chudasama (7)
Krishna Avanti Primary School, Evington

Dear Diary

Today, I went to the park. I went on my scooter but when I got there I saw a sign which told me to find a secret button. I looked everywhere until I found it. It was under the slide and so I pressed it. We got teleported to a new dimension and there were dangerous mutants and they were large colossal giants. I avoided the mutants. Suddenly a boss appeared and it was charging up and got ready to fight. With his special attacks, I decided to fight back and in the end, I won. I was so excited but the portal appeared so I went back to Planet Earth.

Avi Mistry (7)
Krishna Avanti Primary School, Evington

Dear Diary

Let me tell you about an exciting birthday party I went to yesterday. We were celebrating a very special occasion. It was my grandma's birthday. We were so excited. We ate matar paneer, onion mogo mixed with paneer, darr and rice. My aunt, my grandma and my mum were there. It was like a disco there with colourful lights on the ceiling. There was an electric car just like mine. There was a dice cake with dice on it and beautiful decorations and at the end, we watched funny videos and then we had to go and all my aunts had to go too.

Soham Bhutiya (7)
Krishna Avanti Primary School, Evington

Dear Diary

You won't believe what happened to me! Last week, I went to space and sat with my mum, dad and mama on the rocket. It went 10, 9, 8, 7, 6, 5, 4, 3, 2, 1, *zoom!* I was very anxious and extremely scared but excited at the same time!
Then it went up, up, up so fast my seatbelt would have come off but luckily it didn't, phew! On the way, an astronaut popped up and said hello, I waved after it took us to the moon.
I played on the moon and played with my bouncy ball. I had so much fun and then went to bed.

Riya Kumar (7)
Krishna Avanti Primary School, Evington

Dear Diary

Today was the day I was going on a trip. Five minutes before we got there something happened and I randomly disappeared. I didn't understand where I was, I felt very scared. Things were broken and I heard weird noises, it was absolutely terrifying. The class must have been wondering where I was. I thought to myself, *how will I get back?*
I saw an unusual button and pressed it. I snuck out through a passageway. I opened it and it led me back to school. I was so relieved. *Never again*, I thought.

Amber Patel (7)
Krishna Avanti Primary School, Evington

Dear Diary

I had a wonderful day. First I woke up, it was my best friend's birthday so I got dressed, made my bed, brushed my teeth and had breakfast. My mum and dad went to the dentist. It was Saturday 5th June. My mum and dad got back home by 12 then I had to go. My best friend's name is Samar. My other friends went too. We went to a bowling alley. I got 19 pins. After, we got to play in the arcades on lots of different machines. Samar won. We had a very good day. We had a blast, it was super cool!

Kaylan Gohil (7)
Krishna Avanti Primary School, Evington

Dear Diary

It was a lovely and glamorous day so me and my family decided to go to the zoo. There were shops, playgrounds, restaurants and animals. First, we went to the playground. Clumsily I sat down on a bench watching my family play. Suddenly the bench floated up... up... until it started flying. The bench said, "Where do you want to go?"
"Nowhere!" I said.
Then I had an idea. "I want to go where the magic began." Finally, it stopped. I got off and went home.

Aarohi Brahmbhatt (8)
Krishna Avanti Primary School, Evington

Dear Diary

Today, I was on a plane. When the pilot was asleep we started to go down, down, down. Everyone fell in the ocean except me. I fell on an empty island, it was so creepy. One package was a football but the ball was alive. The ball gave me an idea to make a boat. I tried and tried until I made the boat. The whale and seagull helped me and I saw a boat so I said, "Please help me!" and the boat helped me and I came home. I said, "That was the hardest adventure ever!"

Nieve Patel (7)
Krishna Avanti Primary School, Evington

Dear Diary

A few days ago, at the funfair, my brother and sister were going for rides. But when we went on the very last ride it went round and round until we finally ended up in a different world. We had no clue how to get back. Just then we decided to search but there was nothing in sight. Luckily, under a leafy tree, there was a red switch. We didn't know what would happen if we pressed it. After a few minutes we decided to press it and we ended up back at the funfair.

Raya Patel (7)
Krishna Avanti Primary School, Evington

Dear Diary

Today, I went to a gigantic museum but then, when I got to the museum I found the History of Pyramids which was extremely exciting. Next, I saw ancient gods on the ceiling. I wanted to touch them but I couldn't because it was lunchtime so we went to the cafe. I ate a jacket potato and after that, I came back home safely in the car. I played with my toys when I came back home and thought about my day. It was fun thinking about it and that was my exciting day!

Nikunj Sevak (6)
Krishna Avanti Primary School, Evington

Dear Diary

Today, I had a magical adventure with my friend. We saw a magic door and then we opened the door and went inside. Suddenly a unicorn, fairy and a mermaid jumped out and they said, "Welcome to our magic land." We fell down with amazement. Then we had a party and ate some cake that the fairies made and a cupcake that the mermaids made and drank a cup of juice that the unicorns made. Then we had to leave. We were sad that we had to leave.

Radhika Szamocka (7)
Krishna Avanti Primary School, Evington

Dear Diary

Two weeks ago I went to space. I brushed and showered, my parents booked a taxi. It took exactly half an hour. Once we were there I put my suit, my tank and helmet on and went to the rocket. I sat in it and it zoomed off. It went so fast that my seatbelt nearly fell off. I was going to the moon. It was hard to drive a big rocket. When I was there I started to play. After a very, very long time, I came home. It was night so I went to sleep.

Adi Jani (7)
Krishna Avanti Primary School, Evington

Dear Diary

Today, I had the most exciting day because I got sucked into the TV. It took me to the parched savannah. I saw my friend, Avi. We decided to take photos of brilliant animals. Suddenly out jumped a fierce lion. We thought it was harmless but we were wrong. It chased us all around the savannah so we jumped into a bush nervously but the lion slipped into the stream. Me and Avi took our chance and ran as fast as we could and escaped.

Mohan Lokesh (6)
Krishna Avanti Primary School, Evington

Dear Diary

Yesterday was the creepiest day of my life. I went out for a walk in the night. I stopped near a tree and then something caught my eye and I slowly turned my head to the left. I saw a creepy-looking house so I stood up and walked towards it. I stopped where it was and it was not a house, it was a museum. I curiously went in it. I saw the pieces of history. I saw a gem. I touched it. I disappeared. I touched it again. I came back.

Kushal Desai (7)
Krishna Avanti Primary School, Evington

Dear Diary

A few months ago, I went to the park. I went with my mum, dad and sister. I was excited. We went in the car. It was a bright day. We set off in the afternoon. We went on the colourful slide. After that, we had a snack. The snack was very nice. We went on the swings. We took turns pushing each other. We played some more. In the evening we came home in the car. I had a great time at the park.

Srijit Choudhuri (7)
Krishna Avanti Primary School, Evington

Dear Diary

Today, I had the best day of my life. I went to the exquisite funfair with my best friend, Jaslyn. We went on the amazing rides and had a picnic near a massive tree. My favourite one was the pirate ship because it gave me butterflies in my belly. Before we left we bought some hot, delicious doughnuts with sugar on and ate them all up. It was so fun. I'll never forget today!

Aashika Anand (7)
Krishna Avanti Primary School, Evington

Dear Diary

Last week, I went to a football match with my mum, dad and brother, we went in the car. We won the first game, the first game was good. I did a sic header. In the second game, we nearly won. We nearly scored 20 goals but they saved one, they scored 20 goals, we scored 19. In the third game, we won. I hit another sick header. It was an amazing day at the football match.

Shivam Dhamecha (7)
Krishna Avanti Primary School, Evington

Dear Diary

At the weekend, I went to a party with my whole family. I walked because the house we were going to is near to us. When we got to the house we played Roblox and the games we played were 'Flee the Facility' and 'Epic Mindgames'. Then I ate pasta that tasted cheesy. Then we came home at 6 o'clock and I went to sleep. It was a fun day at the party.

Aarna Patel (6)
Krishna Avanti Primary School, Evington

Dear Diary

Yesterday, I went to space. I went with my best friend, David. The first thing we did was to sit on the rocket ship. Then I launched into space and went to the big, bright moon. When we got there we opened the door and went out to have some great fun. Then we saw an alien who gave us two moon rocks and finally, we went home. What a great day we had in space!

Pranav Patel (7)
Krishna Avanti Primary School, Evington

Dear Diary

At the weekend, I went to Skegness with my family. I had the best day of my life. I went to the seaside. There I saw a shop and we bought two lollipops. As we came out of the shop we played in the sand. Mum said, "It's time to go home."
At home, we played lots of games like hide-and-seek and played on our iPads.

Tia Odedra (6)
Krishna Avanti Primary School, Evington

Dear Diary

On Sunday, I went to the funfair. It was fun. I went with my best friend, Jasmine. We both went on a big fun ride. Jasmine was excited. After, we went on another ride, it was much higher. I said, "Let's go on another ride."
She said, "Okay."
Then it got late so we came back home together.

Ania Chauhan (7)
Krishna Avanti Primary School, Evington

Dear Diary

Today, I was walking to the park. As I was walking I saw a monster! It hated people. I was frightened. Me and my family ran as fast as cheetahs. Soon we returned to the house. When I returned home I told my grandma about the ferocious monster that hated humans. I told her about us running away and how we escaped.

Mia Gohil (6)
Krishna Avanti Primary School, Evington

Dear Diary

Last week, me and my best friend, Ania, both went to the park. Also, me and Ania went on the climbing frame but it was a bit of a long way to get to the top of the climbing frame. Soon, me and Ania got to the top! "Yay!" said Ania. "That was so, so good!"
The best day ever!

Jasmine Budwal (7)
Krishna Avanti Primary School, Evington

Dear Diary

Yesterday, I went to space loudly, in 10, 9, 8, 7, 6, 5, 4, 3, 2, 1... blast-off! The rocket went to the moon. There was me and Mehul falling on the moon. Me and Mehul saw a superhero in space. It was awesome. It was soon time to come back to Earth.
See you tomorrow, Diary.

Dhruva Devabala (7)
Krishna Avanti Primary School, Evington

Dear Diary

Today was an amazing day. I went to London to see my aunty, she has lots of beautiful plants. I went to the park, it was so fun, there was a tunnel slide and a zip wire. I went to the shop to buy groceries. It was very hot so I got some ice cream and then I went back home.

Keya Tailor (7)
Krishna Avanti Primary School, Evington

Dear Diary

Yesterday, when I was coming back from school with my family we arrived at the park. I saw my friend, Adi. I asked my parents if I could play with him and they said yes so I did. We played football then we came home. I dreamt of an alien and it was the best day of my life!

Dylan Bhundia (7)
Krishna Avanti Primary School, Evington

Dear Diary

I went on the go-karts and the helter-skelter ride. There were toys and pictures. There were toy boxes in the garden, it was fun. There were sparklers. I went to meet Captain America and he had stars on his back. It was the best day of my life!

Shay Pankhania (6)
Krishna Avanti Primary School, Evington

Dear Diary

At the weekend, I went to my friend's house. We played and ate pizza. We went to the park. At the park, we went on the slide and swings and we climbed on a climbing frame. We ate lots of food and had a great day!

Siya Odedara (7)
Krishna Avanti Primary School, Evington

Dear Diary

Yesterday, I went to the park with my family. I went on a bus. I saw an ice cream van. It was red, yellow and blue then I had an ice cream. It was chocolate and it was tasty! Then we came home and I went to sleep.

Kian Peshawaria (6)
Krishna Avanti Primary School, Evington

Dear Diary

You won't believe this... I know how to swim! My legs are quite small but I learned an easy way. It was a deep pool but my dad helped me. It felt like warm water and I had a good time.

Veda-Shruti Mistry (7)
Krishna Avanti Primary School, Evington

Dear Diary

At the weekend, I played with my friend on Roblox and we met on Google Classroom. We had fun together. We played and we had fun.

Hanaya Kotecha (7)
Krishna Avanti Primary School, Evington

Dear Diary

This week is amazing because it's sports week! We have special, fantastic, fun sports to do every day. How great! We're doing different kinds of sports. Monday morning, our first activities were to go on the bouncy castles. Surprisingly, there were three massive, colourful bouncy castles. Did you know that there was a huge, black and yellow bouncy castle that had a gigantic wrecking ball attached to it? You had to push the ball to knock people off! It was so hard. I felt scared that I was going to get knocked off. I thought that I would fall off but I still had fun. In the afternoon, we played tennis. Did you know that it was odd because we didn't have tennis rackets? We had to use unusual yellow foam gloves and hit the ball. I felt that it was very difficult. I thought that I would break the bat!

On Tuesday, we played cricket. A bowler, called Jack, did the bowling. We all got to do batting and fielding. I hit the ball at least three times. It was awesome! Now I cannot wait to do sports on Friday!

Zara Imran (7)
Lever Edge Primary Academy, Bolton

Dear Diary

Today was a fantastic day in school because it is sports week. We have fun and exciting activities all week, it's awesome! We're having lots of fun. In sports week we have really special fun. On Monday morning, our first activity was to go on a huge, colourful, fun bouncy castle. Surprisingly, there were three giant bouncy castles! We could go on any! There was an extraordinary bouncy castle that had a huge, heavy wrecking ball that pushed us out. The ball was attached to the castle! I pushed people down the bouncy castle! I pushed everyone off it! I had lots of fun. Luckily, I could go on all different types of them. A few hours later, we played tennis, it was a bit unusual and weird because we didn't have tennis rackets! We had to use foam bats to hit the ball.

My partner hit me in the face twice but I was very good at it! I can't wait to see what will happen next!

Wei Qi Chen (7)
Lever Edge Primary Academy, Bolton

Dear Diary

This week is sports week and I'm loving it! We have special fun, amazing activities every single day. The first thing we did was go on bouncy castles. We didn't know that there were going to be three! There was a weird one that had a huge, heavy wrecking ball that we swung to knock people off, I kept falling off. I felt happy because I kept knocking people off. In the afternoon we played tennis but it was different, we had foam bats. I kept hitting the ball everywhere. On Tuesday we played cricket, we had to bat the ball and we got points but we only had one chance. I was the first person to hit it! Yesterday we played football. I kept falling down, I had so much fun! Today we played dodge ball, I didn't get hit much but someone did hit me in the head.

I was out once then I was back in then I hit someone. Tomorrow is yoga, I love yoga!

Aisha Waqar (7)
Lever Edge Primary Academy, Bolton

Dear Diary

This week is sports week and it's amazing. We've had lots of amazing things to do every day. On Monday morning, we went on a bouncy castle. There were three different types of castles. They were colourful and big. One had a ball attached to it. But you had to push the ball hard to push the person off the bouncy castle. One was small but it was still fun. After that, we played tennis. It was weird because we had foam gloves. I was so good and so was Hasan. I liked how Hasan played. I loved tennis.
On Tuesday, we played cricket, it was so fun, the bat was blue.
On Wednesday, we played football, it was so fun.

Lama Abo (7)
Lever Edge Primary Academy, Bolton

Dear Diary

This week is sports week. It's fantastic and awesome because we have done fun, exciting activities. On Monday morning, we went on three gigantic bouncy castles. They were so bright and fun to bounce on. One of them was a special bouncy castle, it had a ball going in circles. I needed to try to get the other people to fall down so I could win but it was hard because it was very heavy. I almost fell down.

On Tuesday, we played cricket. We played cricket in a different way. We had a small ball with a rubber band tied to it. There was an enormous puddle so it was hard to play. I wonder what will happen next?

Adeena Ishaq (7)
Lever Edge Primary Academy, Bolton

Dear Diary

This week is sports week. We have special activities every day, it's exciting and awesome. On Monday morning, there were three huge, gigantic bouncy castles and we could go on any. There was one that had a ball attached to it. It was heavy, the colour was yellow and black. In the afternoon we played tennis but it was a bit different because we had foam bats. I was not good at it but Nali helped me out. On Tuesday, we played cricket, it was fun but it was difficult. Then we played football and we were on the orange team. I was the goalkeeper.

Haidar Khan (7)
Lever Edge Primary Academy, Bolton

Dear Diary

Yesterday, we went to the fair. We had lots of jolly fun. Then we decided to design our own sweets! We're still doing it! It was lunchtime, so I ordered a milkshake with marshmallows, a burger from Burger King and blue candyfloss. After that, me and my monster went swimming, horse riding and did art. After we finished I went to see my friends, Amber and Matilda. We played football, we played with slime and then slept.

Eliza Kotti (6)
Plantation Primary School, Halewood

Dear Diary

Yesterday, we arrived on holiday and it's a place called Grancan area. It was hot and nice at night when we arrived in the lovely colourful place. This morning, we went to the shops and I bought a doll and went with my nan. Then we found a hidden park and we played in it. Soon, we ate and drank some delicious food and drink. Finally, we went swimming and I went in the deep part and ate sweets and chocolate.

Chloe Budd (7)
Plantation Primary School, Halewood

Dear Diary

I asked my mum and dad if we could go to the funfair and they said yes so me and my family went to the funfair yesterday. We went and I packed so many things because it was a ten-hour drive. My mum shouted, "Come on, let's go!" When we got there I saw a big gnome ride. When we got out of the car I found a secret tunnel and there were chocolate milkshakes. Then I found treasure, I was so excited!

Amber Duffy (7)
Plantation Primary School, Halewood

Dear Diary

I went to Wales with my Auntie Sharon, Loren, Kyle and Jaden. We went to the funfair and I went on Wild River and the Batman. I went on the Hungry Caterpillar, it spins and it was scary and fun.

The next day, we played on the beach, had a water fight and at lunchtime, I got a big juicy burger and chips with ketchup, it was delicious. I had a chocolate milkshake and an ice cream too!

Cianna Rainey (7)
Plantation Primary School, Halewood

Dear Diary

Yesterday it was Christmas Eve and I went to my nan's. I opened my presents from my nan. I got a lava lamp and a big cuddly panda that was really furry. Then we had lunch. We had roast chicken and vegetables. We came back home. Santa came and I got a Nintendo Switch and a gaming chair and my brother got the games for the Switch.

Chloe Williams (8)
Plantation Primary School, Halewood

Dear Diary

Two days ago, I went to the fair with my friend. Me and My friend had loads of fun. We went on the spaceship ride, it was scary. At lunchtime, we went to the café. I got a chocolate milkshake and my friend got a strawberry milkshake, it was delicious. I also took my dog and he was trying to drink my yummy milkshake!

Matilda Bate (7)
Plantation Primary School, Halewood

Dear Diary

Yesterday, I went to the fair with Eliza and Amber. Then we went to a party and I ate doughnuts. It was a unicorn party and we played games and dressed up as unicorns. The boys dressed up as dragons and they went to the shops. They went swimming and we went to my friend's house. I had tea and I slept there.

Nylah Ritchie (7)
Plantation Primary School, Halewood

Dear Diary

On my birthday, me and my family went to Legoland and I was so excited. After four hours, we got to the hotel and the next day we went, the journey was forty minutes. We stood for about three hours. We went on five rides and I got a sword, a shield and a teddy. Before we left we went to get some chocolate.

Luca Jones (7)
Plantation Primary School, Halewood

Dear Diary

Today I went through a secret tunnel. At first, I was nervous but I went in. Inside, there was a magical land of chocolate, unicorns, tigers, mermaids and fairies. Wow! It was good! The fairy called Beaty told me, "Come to Fairy Magical Palace and your dreams will come true."

Alice Logan (7)
Plantation Primary School, Halewood

Dear Diary

I went to Chester Zoo when I was four or five. I went with mum, dad and my sister. I saw a tiger, a hippo, a rhino and even a giraffe. It was so tall that his head nearly popped out of the ceiling! I was so brave because I went to the bat cave, it was so scary.

Robyn Ross-Forth (6)
Plantation Primary School, Halewood

Dear Diary

I went to Amber's party and came home then I went to swimming class. My mum left and my auntie came. I had a sleepover. In the morning, we made slime and went to the cinema to watch Peter Rabbit 2. Then my auntie brought me back home.

Evelyn McNally (6)
Plantation Primary School, Halewood

Dear Diary

Five weeks ago, I went to Wales with my family and we went in the car then we were in a camper van. On Saturday and Sunday, we went swimming. I needed armbands and a float. Then we found another float for my brother. I almost drowned.

Evie Sunners (7)
Plantation Primary School, Halewood

Dear Diary

At the weekend, me and my amazing family went to the fair and rode on a dragon. We saw dinosaurs then we went to the shops and got a milkshake and also got sweets, chocolate and a smoothie and after that, we played at the park.

Jack Mcstein (7)
Plantation Primary School, Halewood

Dear Diary

Yesterday, my family and I went to the funfair. It was so fun and we went on the big roller coaster. It made my tummy go funny because it tipped upside down and we went on the Ferris wheel, it was massive!

Bobby Steele (7)
Plantation Primary School, Halewood

Dear Diary

Yesterday, I went to the fair and it was a sunny day. I found a secret tunnel and I explored it, it was dark. I played on the rides and it was fun. There were also horse-riding races.

Sofia Bayliss (7)
Plantation Primary School, Halewood

Dear Diary

At the weekend, I went to Wales on holiday with my new friend. My friend's name is Alice. I drank a huge milkshake and when it was night-time, I went to sleep.

Heidi Hanson (7)
Plantation Primary School, Halewood

Dear Diary

Today I am having a swimming party. I am getting dressed now. I have put on my party clothes. I have got a glittery dress on. I am at the party now. There are buckets and buckets of slime, milkshakes and smoothies.

Romilly Withers (7)
Thornborough Infant School, Thornborough

Dear Diary

I got up really early and went to catch the coach. My football team all travelled on the coach then we arrived at Leyton Orient FC. We came out of a big tunnel and it was exciting, there was a big crowd then we played our first game.

I was running with the ball and I did a stepover to trick the defender and then I kicked the ball and I scored a goal. The game seemed to go so quickly, the next minute the whistle had gone and the game was over, we won 1-0.

In the next game, I got side-tackled in the penalty box. My friend took the penalty and scored. We won the next two games and got into the final. In the final it was very tricky, tackles were flying in. I passed to my friend and he scored a great goal in the top corner. The other team equalised and I felt sad. I knew I needed to do something special.

I started to run with the ball, I nutmegged two players and then clipped the ball over the goalkeeper and scored! The crowd cheered, "Harley! Harley!" That meant the best thing, my team won the tournament. We were all so excited, I lifted the trophy as high as I could.

Harley Craig (7)
Upminster Infant School, Upminster

Dear Diary

Today, the most unbelievable thing happened. I was on the train on my way to Wembley Stadium when I saw a trail of slime in the carriage. It was green and glittery. I wondered where it had come from so I followed it. It led to the back seat. There sitting was a slimy, lumpy monster! I was shocked but he was smiling so I said, "Hello." The monster said, "I am going to Wembley to watch the England football match against Germany."
I said, "Me too," so we went together. When we got there we felt hungry so we went to get some snacks. I got a hot dog and a smoothie, but Scruff got ten of each and had eaten them before we sat down. The game started, it was very exciting. At the final whistle, it was 2-0 to England. Raheem Sterling and Harry Kane scored one goal each. Harry Kane threw his shirt into the crowd but the monster ate it! Soon it was time to go home.

We both said goodbye and agreed to watch England versus Ukraine in the quarter-final together and I said I would bring him lots of snacks!

Oliver Humphrey (7)
Upminster Infant School, Upminster

Dear Diary

As part of my seventh birthday, my parents took me on a staycation break to Dorset. We got to stay in a beautiful hotel in Bournemouth and I loved how the hotel staff gave me birthday balloons when we arrived.

The next morning, we went on a fascinating, fossil hunting trip to Lyme Regis. When we got there, I was mesmerised by the view of the rocky, pebble beach, and the glistening sun dancing on top of the sea. The weather was just perfect, bright, sunny-hot with a cool, calm breeze.

We met with a fabulous fossil guide who taught us more about fossils in Lyme Regis and how to search for them. I was so excited and couldn't wait to start looking for real fossils. We got to learn that Mary Anning discovered the first complete ichthyosaurus fossil in England and she was just twelve years old at the time.

I began searching under the rocks carefully and happily found some ammonite fossils. I had the best birthday ever and really hope to go back there again. Maybe one day I will become a palaeontologist!

Kaya Shah (7)
Upminster Infant School, Upminster

Dear Diary

Today, I was playing Minecraft. Suddenly, there was a flash of light and the room went pitch-black. All I could see was the Minecraft logo. I looked around me and saw brown, green, pink, blue, orange, red and purple squares everywhere. I saw my Minecraft house, but it wasn't the size it is on the computer screen... it was the size of my own house!
Another Minecraft player started talking to me. It sounded like my sister, Millie. She was in the game too. She shouted, "Run!"
A hoard of creepers were after us. I got my pickaxe out of my backpack and started digging a hole to hide. I dug and dug. Next, I was hit on the head by an Enderman that fell down the hole. I was stuck. I heard Millie shouting and I saw holes in the wall of dirt. Millie was coming through. She got a ladder and we both climbed out. I climbed and climbed and climbed out of the game.

The next thing I knew, I was back on the sofa but Millie was not there. She was still in the game! Tomorrow I have to save her!

Iggy Cox (7)
Upminster Infant School, Upminster

Dear Diary

I went to an unknown planet where I found out there were lava oceans and no water. I thought I was on the Black Planet, home to Crustiana, an evil beast who has destroyed planets. I looked at the lava oceans and saw a strange monster. It looked like a Skullcrawler but bigger. It had giant claws and razor teeth. It roared and the Crustiana was summoned.

I defeated the dragon with my snow blaster. When I started to run the monster roared again. I then realised it was summoning the Crustania king. It started to chase me. I got to my spaceship and flew away. When I got home, I decided to name the monster the Lavaviathen.

The next day, I saw a red building in the distance. I got there and I realised it was abandoned. I opened it and realised there were zombies. They soon walked away and I saw a strange room.

I walked in and saw cool weapons. I took all of them and walked out.
It was getting really dark and the candle was almost out. I'll go back soon.

George Jaques (7)
Upminster Infant School, Upminster

Dear Diary

This was the most unexpected day ever! When I woke up this morning, I read the local newspaper and there had been reports of bright lights shining over the woods. Those woods are right behind my house. I had to find out more about the lights so I set off as fast as I could to the woods. It was dark and creepy. I climbed over a fallen tree trunk and on the other side was a cave! I crawled through the small entrance that had a drawing of a gem scratched into the wall. At the end of the tunnel, I saw a green light. I walked closer to the light and I saw something that I had only seen in books - a huge gem! I touched it and I felt power running through my body. Suddenly, from the shadows of the cave came zombies that were guarding the gem. I turned to run and I was able to run as fast as lightning. The gem gave me super cool powers.

Once I was out of the cave, I jumped over the tree trunk but instead of landing on the floor, I was flying! Best day ever!

Parker Brannigan Warren (7)
Upminster Infant School, Upminster

Dear Diary

A pretty little mermaid called Jess lives under the sea and swims in the magically clear water. She peeps her head out and wishes she could be like everyone else in the city. This mermaid is me. Sometimes I want to be like everyone else. My friend, Reeva, has three bulldogs and likes to take them on a walk to the park as I would love to have a little dog. My other friend, Avaani has a little sister but she doesn't like the magical clear water where I live, the sea is like my home. I am very lucky to have a big brother. He helped me carry the heavy Lego box and played with me, throwing and catching the squashie. I look after my cousin's dog called Molly. My mum and dad look after me and love me a lot. I have ten friends and have a nice teacher called Miss Sterling. I don't need to be like anyone else, I just want to be myself and no one else.

Lottie Hindley (7)
Upminster Infant School, Upminster

Dear Diary

Today, me and Oliver went to a big zoo. When we got there we parked our red Ferrari then went inside where we found a stripy orange and back tiger having a nap. Next, we followed the long wavy path to a black and white bamboo-loving panda eating bamboo up a very tall tree.
Me and Oliver then went to a café and had a giant chocolate chip ice cream with a cherry on top. After, we paid lots of money to ride on elephants, all around the zoo, going slowly so we could see all the animals. My favourite was the hippo wallowing in the dirty swamp. Oliver asked the elephants to throw us into the penguin pool so we could go for a long cool swim with the playful penguins and then we drove back in our red, fast Ferrari to the Tower of London where we live.

Albie Dickinson (7)
Upminster Infant School, Upminster

Dear Diary

One day in the Easter holidays, I found my dad working at the end of the garden with a gigantic digger! I wanted to help so I did and it was monumentally fun! That night, I almost fell asleep on the sofa. The next day, I was so excited, I fell out of bed. I got to work straight away. I clambered on and started the engine. It clanged and banged and clanged and banged. It bashed its way across the boards and into the back of the garden. I rumbled towards the old rusty shed and slowly lifted the digger arm. *This*, I thought, *is going to be fun.* I looked at my dad and he gave me the thumbs up so I pushed the lever right and then left and the shed exploded into a million tiny pieces. I couldn't believe it. I had demolished a shed!

Jack Fryer (7)
Upminster Infant School, Upminster

Dear Diary

On Sunday, I was with my best friend, Harley. We went to the zoo. There were tigers, lions and even dolphins but I was terrified. I looked behind me and there was a terrifying, huge monster so we ran to my safe house but the monster chased me but before he could get in I locked the door. Harley and I waited in silence for hours. The monster didn't go until the next day. My sleep was terrible, all I could think about was the huge monster. We went back and there was no monster and Harley went home and saw the monster. He was scarier, it was green with dark orangey eyes, it was humongous. Harley got a knife and stabbed it. The monster was still alive, he did it over and over again. He still didn't die. He could never die.

Ben (7)
Upminster Infant School, Upminster

Dear Diary

I went to Stubbers with my family and friends. Stubbers is an outdoor adventure park. There was a tunnel leading to the playground. There was a steep, tall climbing frame that guided us to a secret hideout. Once it had stopped raining we took a pedalo ride on the murky, green lake. We took turns to pedal and steer the pedalo. After we went on the pedalo we went to the play park. At the play park, we went on the monkey bars and there was some rope that we had to balance on. It was quite hard but I did it. Then we went back to my house. My friend made cookies with my mum. They were delicious! Then they had to leave to go and watch football. I had the best day with my friends.

Isabel Burdett (7)
Upminster Infant School, Upminster

Dear Diary

Once, I went to the beach and got in the sea. When I got in the sea, suddenly, I became a... mermaid! I had a scaly blue fishy tail and a sequin seashell bra. I had beautiful make-up and beautiful brown, straight hair to blonde beautiful hair. I went off to find something new.
I swam under rocks and above rocks. I saw turtles, whales, dolphins and... a shark! I swam away as quickly as I could. I hid in a deep, dark shipwreck. It swam above me and when it was gone I came out slowly and looked around. It had gone so I crept out and swam back to the bay. And just then, I changed back to normal old me. I had a wonderful adventure!

Ellie Winston (7)
Upminster Infant School, Upminster

Dear Diary

I went to Legoland with my friends and family. The park is full of amazing rides. I was very brave when I went on a new ride that was called Sky Lion. Sky Lion felt like you were travelling through a different world. There were incredible animals flying around. I felt like I was flying too. My mum was screaming. My favourite ride was Mia's Adventure. This ride feels like you are falling with a horse. It goes up and down and spins. We had food at Bricks Restaurant. I had a beef burger. It was delicious. We played in the playground with our friends and then went to bed. We were tired from the long day.

Sophia Aherne (7)
Upminster Infant School, Upminster

Dear Diary

I am soon going to a party. We are going to paint animal pottery. We can choose any animal we want. We can choose out of thirty different colours. We will be having yummy Fruit Shoots and orange squash and Ribena and lots of Party Rings in white, pink and purple. Also, we are going to have yummy strawberries, loads of Hula Hoops, cheese and jam sandwiches and breadsticks. Suddenly, Mr Blobby rang the doorbell and we had loads of fun. And before we knew it the party was over. Everyone went. Mr Blobby was running at the pottery because they looked so nice and chased them all the way to the fireplace.

Joseph Walters (7)
Upminster Infant School, Upminster

Dear Diary

Today, me and my best friend went to a super funfair. There was a stripy red and white circus. Inside were cool acrobats walking on skinny tightropes. I loved the big Ferris wheel. The view from the top was fantastic, we could see the whole funfair. There was a swing roundabout that spun really fast and made us very dizzy. At lunchtime we ate a hot dog and candyfloss, it was delicious. My daddy played a game where you throw balls at coconuts. He was really good and knocked them all down, he won me a gargantuan teddy. I was so happy.
It was a lovely day and I had the best time ever.

Jaden Thurston (7)
Upminster Infant School, Upminster

Dear Diary

Today, I went to the adventure park with my family and my friend, Robyn. We went on the Scorpion ride which was very fast. Robyn and I loved the laser show with the laser guns shooting at the fire-spitting dragon. My brother, Sebastian, had a great time at the mini zoo and the tractor ride. We had hot dogs with chips and a lot of ice cream. In the evening, we had our dinner with the Gruffalo. He wasn't scary at all. After our delicious meal, we slept in a huge tent. The whole day was very exciting. I would love to go back soon!

Torben Barr (6)
Upminster Infant School, Upminster

Dear Diary

I went to my nanny's exquisite house for a sleepover and it was for twenty nights. I went on my own for twenty nights but I took every single one of my teddies! It was scary until I faced my fear for the whole night and after that, I got ice cream because I am only six years old. Sometimes if I was good and brave as well Nanny would buy me a present like L.O.L.s and if I didn't want a toy she would get me sweets like Sour Patches Kids, marshmallows, sour Haribos or maybe fruit and tomatoes. After that, I went home.

Reeva King (6)
Upminster Infant School, Upminster

Dear Diary

At the weekend, I went to the woods with my friend, Sophia. As we were picking roses together I saw a dark red glow through the bright green trees. I thought I saw roses but as I got closer I saw it was not roses, it was bright red fire squirting up. I tried to warn Sophia but she was not there. I was trapped in the thorny bushes. I was very frightened. It was coming closer and closer then I saw it was a wild Pokémon and its name was Ponyta. Ponyta belonged to no one so I became her Pokémon master.

Freya Webb (7)
Upminster Infant School, Upminster

Dear Diary

Me and my best friend were going home from holiday on a boat but suddenly, we bumped into a desert island. We jumped out of the boat and saw that there was a humongous hole in it. Then my friend came up with an idea. The idea was that we start making a home on the desert island. So that's what we did. It was very tiring building the house but we did it in four months. Once we built the house we saw someone calling to us. They got closer and they said, "Jump on!" so we did and we got home safely.

Hollie Kitchener (7)
Upminster Infant School, Upminster

Dear Diary

I went to Splashland with a colourful, silly monster. We did some art and licked a vanilla bubblegum lollipop. It was delicious! My favourite bit was when we went down a water slide, with food colouring in the water. We met a Lego person with a smiley face and red eyes. His name was Duplo. He liked eating Lego bricks. We saw a fearsome red tiger with sharp beady tusks who chased us. At the end of the day, we went home on the big back of the tiger together. It was a great day!

Henry Davidson (6)
Upminster Infant School, Upminster

Dear Diary

Today at 4 o'clock, I went to my drama class and played lots of fun games. When drama was finished I went back to my grandparents' house and played in a secret tunnel they'd bought for me (until it broke). For dinner, I ate sausages, chips and peas with lashings of ketchup and for dessert, I had a big chunk of apple pie. When I went home my parents set up my tent in the garden and we watched a movie. Finally, we went to sleep under the stars.

Cecily Lloyd (6)
Upminster Infant School, Upminster

Dear Diary

Today, I went to the park and found a secret tunnel that was hidden in the middle of a tree. When I climbed inside I found an alien crying because his spaceship had broken down. Behind him was a little red Pokémon named Fluffball. The alien asked for help fixing his spaceship and I said yes. I pressed the big black reset button and the ship started to move. The alien and his Pokémon waved and they flew away.

Sienna Woodhurst (7)
Upminster Infant School, Upminster

Dear Diary

Today, I went on a magical adventure with my sister, Isabella. I landed on an island, it was mysterious. I was very worried, so was Isabella. We comforted ourselves by holding each other's hands. Suddenly, we saw a tail jump out of the sea. It was a mermaid. I was surprised because I haven't seen one in my life. I ran up to the sea to see the mermaid. It swam up to me. "My name is Annie," she said.

Xanthia Groom (7)
Upminster Infant School, Upminster

Dear Diary

Yesterday, I went to the funfair with my friends and family. On the way, I got McDonald's and on my Nintendo, I played Minecraft with my friends. We got ice cream when we finished our McDonald's. When we arrived we went on all the rides. When we were finished we went to the arcade. We had lots of tickets and lots of fun. My favourite ride was the roller coaster and my favourite game was basketball.

Harry Cheek (7)
Upminster Infant School, Upminster

Dear Diary

I had a fantastic weekend. On Friday evening, I started at Upminster Cricket Club. I liked fielding the most. On Saturday, my dad took me to Smyths Toy Superstore in Romford. My dad bought me a Bakugan toy. Afterwards, we walked to Raphael Park. I had a nice ice cream. Someone locked the main gate and we had to find another way out. Daddy was very cross. I also played rugby today.

David Ryan (7)
Upminster Infant School, Upminster

Dear Diary

Today, I woke up with butterflies in my tummy. I was so excited as it was my brother, Joseph's fifth birthday party. Mummy had decorated the house with balloons and banners. Joseph got lots of presents. His favourite was the Lego train set. Afterwards, the doorbell rang and it was his friends. There was pizza and a train cake. The party was amazing.

Emily Walder (7)
Upminster Infant School, Upminster

Dear Diary

Yesterday, we met our friends at the river. We hired a boat for an hour and Daddy crashed into a tree and I had to duck. The cows went for a swim in the river too. We were under a tree in a field in a thunderstorm. We got soaked, it felt like a shower. My shoe fell off because it was so slippery. I ran upstairs and went to have a warm shower when I got home.

Poppy Fleet (7)
Upminster Infant School, Upminster

Dear Diary

When we got to Legoland we had fun on the bumper cars. Then we went on the rollercoasters, it was very fast and big. After, we had some food. I had seven chicken nuggets, they were delicious! After a busy day, we went to the hotel and went into our room. We sat down and watched TV.
Tomorrow we are going to play carnival games.

Eniola Orisatoki (6)
Upminster Infant School, Upminster

Dear Diary

I have a secret. I saw Father Christmas but he didn't see me. I woke up in the night. I got out of my bed when I heard a noise down the stairs. I went downstairs and he was in the living room putting presents under the tree. The Christmas elves saw me and chased me back to bed. I was sad that I didn't meet him.

Joshua Quilter (6)
Upminster Infant School, Upminster

Dear Diary

I went swimming and practised my breaststroke then I went to my nanny and grandad's house. We played in the garden. On Sunday, I went to my grandma's house to play. After, I went to get a milkshake and an ice cream. I chose an Oreo ice cream then I came back home to see my dog, Eddie, and to eat my dinner.

Sophia Crocker (7)
Upminster Infant School, Upminster

Dear Diary

We went to the Tower of London and saw ravens. After that, we went to the gift shop. I got a teddy bear keyring and Henry got a bookmark. I saw the Crown Jewels and I saw a whole dress of jewels and saw a ruby red gem. After that we went to Burger & Lobster, I had a burger then we came home on the train.

Ruby Trew (6)
Upminster Infant School, Upminster

Dear Diary

Today, I went in my TARDIS and visited the dinosaurs and I hid from a gigantosaurus that was chasing me. It ate everyone in its path, only some survived. It destroyed buildings and even ate an elephant. Luckily, I found a horde of angry dinosaurs and defeated it. All the people said, "Phew!"

James Bailey (7)
Upminster Infant School, Upminster

Dear Diary

I went to the zoo with Emily. We saw lots of animals and drank Coca Cola. In the afternoon we decided to do gymnastics, which was lots of fun. We did cartwheels and handstands. The sun was shining very brightly so we wanted to cool down. So me and Emily decided to dive into the local open-air pool.

Eden Mackenzie-Smith (7)
Upminster Infant School, Upminster

Dear Diary

I went to the funfair with my family and had lots of fun. I enjoyed all sorts of rides including 'the fun house' which I went on twice with my cousin, Oscar. I then played 'hook a duck' and won my sister a prize. It was the best day ever, even though it rained and we all got wet.

Finlay Hardy (7)
Upminster Infant School, Upminster

Dear Diary

One pleasant morning, I asked if I could go to the park with Abigail, Zara, Daddy, Mummy and Holly. They all agreed to go to the park. We had a great time there and we went on the monkey bars and the slide, the roundabout, the swing and the sandpit and I made a sandcastle.

Alice Pepper (7)
Upminster Infant School, Upminster

Dear Diary

The day finally came where I got to go to Jamie's party. It was brilliant. There were lots of people, bouncy trampolines, an obstacle course and lots more. Jamie even had a great football cake that we got to have after yummy pizza. It was the best day ever.

Henry Francis (7)
Upminster Infant School, Upminster

Dear Diary

I went to Henry's house yesterday. We got married and I gave rings to Henry and Bella. We made a potion and we put bugs in it. We had chocolate cookies and sweets. Then we played football and catch together. After, we said goodbye and came home.

Lexia Napier Deutsher (7)
Upminster Infant School, Upminster

Dear Diary

I'm going to have a playdate with David on Sunday. I like swimming on Monday with James.
A few weeks ago, I became a mini red ball champion at Grosvenor. Today, Germany played England and England won 2-0 and I played football today in my garden.

Bertram Moore (7)
Upminster Infant School, Upminster

Dear Diary

Yesterday, I went to a football stadium to watch West Ham score a goal. They scored ten goals and after I got a Mini Milk from Stubbers Park. I saw Eevee, it was a type of Pokémon and we had a bubble bath with Eevee.

Freya Bourne (7)
Upminster Infant School, Upminster

Dear Diary

On Sunday, me and my father went to the transport museum. We took lots of pictures and bought some toys. In Boston, we ordered some chips and a burger then we went to Mama's house and then went home.

Kyle Sagisi (6)
Upminster Infant School, Upminster

Dear Diary

I went to the Cotswolds and I went to have breakfast. I had poached eggs on toast and then I got back to the car park and I went to the Cotswolds Wildlife Park with my mummy and daddy. I looked at the rhinos and then we moved on. I saw the camels and a bushbaby. I went to the toilet and then I found my mummy and then we went to the leopards and I saw two of them.

Emin Mehmet-Khan (6)
Wraysbury Primary School, Wraysbury

Dear Diary

I went to my grandma's house on Saturday and I laid down with my grandma's cat, and I went on my bicycle. I went up the hill and down the hill and I jumped on my trampoline. I went to the river next to her back garden. But my cat came along. My cat's name is Billy. Then I chased her. It was a great day.

Zoya Hayat (6)
Wraysbury Primary School, Wraysbury

Dear Diary

I went to get ice cream.
I went to the park and played on the swings.
I played football in the garden.
I went to Wembley Stadium.
I went to play rugby.
I went to my sister's house.
I went to London.
I went to Paddington.
I went to Aidan's house for a playdate.

Kairan Kharay (6)
Wraysbury Primary School, Wraysbury

Dear Diary

I went to my auntie's home and we surprised her. We slept at her house and we watched football. We all wore matching shirts and I had my nails painted. The next day we went to the park. After the park, we went back to have a bath then we went downstairs to have dinner before we went home.

Grace Kirby (6)
Wraysbury Primary School, Wraysbury

Dear Diary

I went to Nicky's house to watch the football, it was really fun and England won. It was exciting. My mum and dad were away and my nan was looking after me, Sienna and Rocky. It was fun and we played Hatchimals and a puppy came round, he was cute. I also went to the park. What did you do?

Beau Loveridge (6)
Wraysbury Primary School, Wraysbury

Dear Diary

I went to Alton Towers with my cousins. I went on my first high ride and we slept inside of the hotel. My favourite ride was the Wicker Man ride and I even got merch. I got a teddy and it was a unicorn. My sister got one gift and I got two gifts.

Sophia Bedford (6)
Wraysbury Primary School, Wraysbury

Dear Diary

I went to my grandma's house and I stayed for a sleepover with my cousin and I went to the funfair. In the morning, I ate pancakes for breakfast, I had syrup on them. At the funfair, I went on a trampoline. What did you do?

Eva Shurman (5)
Wraysbury Primary School, Wraysbury

Dear Diary

Villagers came to my house and played with Lego then went outside and had food. They had chocolate, cake and bread and the villagers gave me a present. If I keep it in water for two years it will turn into a dinosaur!

Aidan Woollard (6)
Wraysbury Primary School, Wraysbury

Dear Diary

On Friday, my aunty came for a sleepover. I stayed up until 10.30, the others stayed up until 00.00.
On Saturday, it was family day and we played coconuts. After lunch, we went to the park.

Harrison Cowie (6)
Wraysbury Primary School, Wraysbury

Dear Diary

I went to the park and I went to The George but all the tables were full so we went to a new pub. Ben had a sleepover. We watched the England match. At 10 o'clock I went to bed.

Lexi Burke (6)
Wraysbury Primary School, Wraysbury

Dear Diary

I went to the play area with my family. It was cool but the time was soon over so I had to go home. My brother was sad so I said we will go again. What have you been doing?

Rehaan Mian (6)
Wraysbury Primary School, Wraysbury

Dear Diary

I went to the toy shop. I got two Ben Ten toys and Luka Funko Pop and a Monster Truck toy. Then I went to McDonald's where I got a triple cheeseburger in a Happy Meal.

Renzo Assi (6)
Wraysbury Primary School, Wraysbury

Dear Diary

I flew Tejj's drone at the park with my dad. I also went to the shops to buy flower seeds then I went to my house. I also played tag with Tejj. Do you know who won?

Ikonkar Gill-Mangat (6)
Wraysbury Primary School, Wraysbury

Dear Diary

I went to the park with my daddy and we had ice cream.
Yesterday, I went to my cousin's house.
Tomorrow, I am going to stay up until midnight.

Azaan Ali (6)
Wraysbury Primary School, Wraysbury

Dear Diary

I went to a hotel with my family and on Sunday, I went to a wedding. I joined the beds together and I watched a football match. We got six presents each.

Priya Basra (6)
Wraysbury Primary School, Wraysbury

Dear Diary

I went to the cinema with my mum and dad to see Zog. Then I went out for lunch at Zizzi and I ate pizza and pasta. I had a good day. What did you do?

Freya McKenzie (6)
Wraysbury Primary School, Wraysbury

Dear Diary

I went to my auntie's house and watched football. England won once again. I drew with my cousins, Ellie, Grace and Savana. I had a lovely time.

Ava Kirby (6)
Wraysbury Primary School, Wraysbury

Dear Diary

I went to the Rose and Crown for my dad's birthday. We had dinner and it was yummy then we went to the park for five minutes. I had cake.

Darcie Taggart (6)
Wraysbury Primary School, Wraysbury

Dear Diary

I went to Durdle Door but it started to rain so we went to a fancy restaurant and I watched the match. When we went out I had a Fruit Shoot.

Rion Agrawal (6)
Wraysbury Primary School, Wraysbury

Dear Diary

On Saturday, I watched the football match and England won 4-0. On Saturday, I also found a shiny shell and I added it to my rock collection.

Ikraj Matharoo (6)
Wraysbury Primary School, Wraysbury

Dear Diary

I went and played with my friend, Katie. She is ten years old. We played for one minute and then I went back home to watch the football.

Lottie Connolly (6)
Wraysbury Primary School, Wraysbury

Dear Diary

I went to a party. I played games and watched a movie then I went to my cousin's and watched another movie.

Luke Richens (6)
Wraysbury Primary School, Wraysbury

Dear Diary

I went to Legoland and I went on the water ride. I got wet on the ride and then I went on the Ninjago ride.

Shaniyal Mahmood (6)
Wraysbury Primary School, Wraysbury

Dear Diary

I went to Alton Towers. There was a water park in the hotel. I had breakfast and I slept on the bunk beds.

Michael Harris (6)
Wraysbury Primary School, Wraysbury

Dear Diary

Me and my daddy watched football. England won. I was happy because England got four goals.

Ralphie Croft (6)
Wraysbury Primary School, Wraysbury

Dear Diary

I had Chinese for dinner. I saw Nyla playing cricket on the green. She was amazing.

Oliwia Lubinska (6)
Wraysbury Primary School, Wraysbury

Young Writers Information

We hope you have enjoyed reading this book – and that you will continue to in the coming years.

If you're a young writer who enjoys reading and creative writing, or the parent of an enthusiastic poet or story writer, visit our website **www.youngwriters.co.uk/subscribe** to join the World of Young Writers and receive news, competitions, writing challenges, tips, articles and giveaways! There is lots to keep budding writers motivated to write!

If you would like to order further copies of this book, or any of our other titles, then please give us a call or order via your online account.

Young Writers
Remus House
Coltsfoot Drive
Peterborough
PE2 9BF
(01733) 890066
info@youngwriters.co.uk

Join in the conversation!
Tips, news, giveaways and much more!

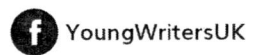

YoungWritersUK   @YoungWritersCW   @YoungWritersCW